GUNSLINGER GREED

Mark Stone

To the love of my life.

Without her, nothing would contain worth.

Not even writing.

CLAUDE THE SPECTER

"Earl Claudius Wade," said the spirit, "time ta fess up. Wad ya do?"

Earl said nothing, but managed to keep staring at Claude the Specter backlit by flames dancing and crackling in the sooty fireplace. He and the ghost shared an exactness right down to a hawkish face, shorn blonde hair, a pair of double-action Colts strapped in holsters, and clothes—tattered britches and gray shirts sweat-stained to near black at the armpits. Like Earl's, Claude's stretched open at the collar to expose a sinewy neck still showing marks from the hanging Earl counted himself lucky to escape.

Perchance, he reckoned, he hadn't fully survived. His mirror-image Claude had appeared moments after the branch broke.

The ghost—seemingly catching his thoughts—glared through close-set eyes. The lifelessness of those brown irises caused Earl to drop his gaze and study the dirt floor of the dilapidated cabin. Spots floated in his vision, similar to after staring at the sun for too long. His body took on the lightness of that hot-air balloon straining to break free of its tethers he saw once at a state fair. He grabbed hold of his Colts' grips. Secured his basket, so to speak.

"Wad ya do?" Claude insisted.

Earl whispered, "Nary a thing the bitch din't deserve. She *needed* ta die."

"Why?"

Because she had sniggered... "Shad-up, Claude."

"She poked fun at yer tally-whacker, din't she, Wade?"

Belinda, she of feathery chocolaty tresses, had possessed boobs that jiggled whenever the whore erupted into laughter. Bitch had never guffawed harder than when Earl dropped his baggy, shit-colored trousers and thrust his hips forward to give Belinda a view of his pecker. Right spooky it was how fast the woman he looked at changed from a shakester of plump features naked and spread-eagled on a bed to a she-pup bouncing and yapping. Could have been one of them doppelgangers in a dime-novel he had struggled to read.

No choice but to bash in Belinda's skull.

That was—what?—two weeks ago her blood splattered his face and tongue.

Claude nodded. "Ya liked the flavor, din't ya?"

Earl rubbed his stiffening member.

"*Good*, huh?" Claude pointed at a window akin to the cabin's every other see-through. The window sported a busted frame from which shards of mucky glass jutted and glowed in the snow-brightened moonlight. "They're out there, the posse. Idjuts, ridin' in the night, horses makin' a ruckus. Hooves poundin' the ground. Thump-thump! Thump-thump! Hellfire, if'n I were deaf and standin' miles afar, I could hear them beasts stomp. Comin' for ya they are, Wade. Watch ya gonna do?"

He yanked his pistols free of their holsters. How the steel whisked against leather and the grips melded with his palms sent a bolt of electricity straight to Earl's hardened manhood. Zest spring-loaded his every muscle.

Time to take on the devils pursuing him.

"Hellhound heathens," he cackled.

"Uh-huh." Claude sashayed his hips. "Put 'em in their graves, Wade. Fuck 'em in their asses 'til they six feet under, pushin' up daisies, catchin' a ride with the ferryman, takin' a dirt nap. Call it how's ya want. Just go on. Send 'em ta Hell ridin' lead!"

Earl whirled and drove his boot heel into the shoddy door. Rotted wood splintered and crashed to the fallen-in porch. Past the mess, he dashed into the teeth-chattering outside, snickering and figuring to paint the snow crimson. Stain the white, twinkling carpet that went uninterrupted by sinister shadows of spooky aspen.

The first of the posse cleared the trees bent over his horse's neck, peashooters popping and hitting everything except Earl, who calmly raised his Colt then squeezed that trigger nice and slow. The bullet found its target, sound redolent of smacking a flabby ass. A few gallops later the slumping rider dropped from the horse that got scared off by another heathen charging into the clearing. This chowderhead was dumb, too, spraying bullets at nothing in particular.

Panic ate at men afraid of dying.

Earl snorted, got off a kill-hit, and waited for the next chump while jigging to a joyous mental tune, recollecting how he panicked his own failure of a mare off a cliff and spewed cum in his britches at the sight.

The more deaths he caused, the looser he got, and by God's heavenly balls, he was ready to be a wind-blown sheet hanging off a clothesline and snapping.

Metal clicked from behind a thick bush. Earl shrugged, shot blind. His luck had always been great for killing. A rifleman stood, moaning, and crumpled onto the branches. The dolt's appaloosa galloped into the open. Earl thought what the shit did it matter and plugged the hoss, too, then spun on the motion caught with the corner of his eye.

Two gents.

Fatty rode a sorrel; Skinny a fine charger. Smart and patient these two. Calm. Though both men's guns bobbed in accordance to their horses' high-stepping trot, the men kept their barrels trained on Earl.

"Wade," the portly fella claimed, "got you dead in our sights."

He let fly a slug as Fatty sent a bullet whizzing by. Earl crouched, threw away a Colt, and fanned the other pistol's hammer with his palm, the smell of spent gunpowder filling his nostrils.

Thumps, groans, and gurgles. Fatty and Skinny stopped breathing.

Claude moseyed up beside him. "Wanna eat watch ya kilt?"

Earl shook his head.

"Dumb, but have it yer way. Fetch us that charger yonder so we can get. Yessir, a vault inside a Deadwood bank requires emptying. May as it happens, a teller will insist on a slug twixt the eyes."

Every decision, when you got to the heart of things, came down to blind chance.

THE CHARGER

Daybreak cast a burnt-orange hue over the forest of pine and aspen while fog swirled around the bottoms of tree-trunks and blanketed the mud. Each time Earl's charger lifted a hoof, there came a sucky pop that held a hypnotizing quality and had him riding leisure-style in the saddle. He let the reins rest on the saddle-horn and put both hands to his hips that lolled in rhythm with the charger's gait. Dreamt of the gold waiting to be stolen in Deadwood. Afterwards he planned hightailing it to California, figured the ocean far enough for evading warrants and—

The hoss stepping in a hole sent a jolt of pain to Earl's lower-back. He stretched out the discomfort, wincing and wrinkling his nose over the stink of his armpits. Awful, yet not as terrible as the rotten-egg odor that wafted on those occasions his ass bounced off the saddle.

What he wouldn't do for a hot-spring.

Nigh on a month since a bath and change of dress. Dunderheaded, him leaving the cabin in such an all-fire hurry. He should have salvaged threads off the posse. Now the clothes went to waste covering bodies that rotted—Earl licked saliva from his lips, unable to recollect when—

"Two days past," muttered Claude floating next to him. "Saloon in Hill City."

"Meal left unfinished." Within minutes of sitting at the eating-table a deputy had spotted him chowing on charcoal masquerading as beef. The deputy hollered, drew his pistol. Earl did likewise. With the lawmen dead, he skedaddled out the saloon and hopped on the no-good mare he later ran off a cliff, hell-bent for the woods. Fun, that ride. Wind in his face, crisp air chilling his snoz. Better than this lollygagging. "Haw!"

The charger bucked and broke into a full run. Branches snagged on Earl's sleeves as the horse slalomed around trees to a bank overlooking a river. He prodded the charger into jumping headlong, the horse whinnying either from his spurs or the prospect of leaping into a creek.

Muddy water flooded Earl's nostrils. Daylight dimmed when he and the horse sank, re-brightened upon their breaking the surface. He heeled the charger's ribs to get it moving; needless because the animal was smart enough to swim, but blast the heavens, him being a taskmaster, he couldn't help giving it a push. Just for good measure, Earl swung a roundhouse punch and popped the steed's neck.

That got them quick to the far bank where the charger hoofed the wall, taking healthy chunks of earth in reaching dry land.

Weren't time for a breather.

Earl smacked the charger with a flattened palm and whipped it with the reins side-to-side. The snaps sent tingles up his spine. He spurred and kept spurring, ignored the pine needles poking him and turned a deaf ear and blind eye to the hoss's wheezing and slobbering; signs the steed neared exhaustion. A pity he lost his knife somewhere along the way; a few stabs with a Bowie blade in the steed's haunch would make the thing run until life left its body.

"Earl-boy," Pa had been fond of saying, "ain't no time for dillydallying. Find yourself lazin', 'member this. Pure cussedness carries a man twice farther than any hoss and is three times more pleasin' than a whore's pussy."

THE CHARGER

In his mind Earl heard the familiar crack of Pa's whip, felt the whip slice into his back. Nope, shouldn't have delayed chopping firewood. Could be ole dad might show up in the here and now to chastise him for taking it easy given Claude made the journey from the netherworld.

Earl again slugged the horse's neck and bellowed, "C'mon, bitch. Neither Pa nor nobody showed me none o' mercy. I'll be damned if'n I give ya any."

The charger succumbed miles after the river. He tried abiding the recuperation, but patience was a distant relative. With the sun overhead—'bout noontime, Earl reckoned—he slid from the saddle and moseyed around front to pinch the horse's snout and yank its head so he could peer into a circular eye. Behind the long eyelashes glimmered a lake of golden-brown. In the middle was a toothpick-shaped island of black. Earl drew out a Colt and put the revolver to the charger's noggin.

"There-there," he cooed.

And pulled the trigger.

III

THE GULCH

Clouds puffed out Earl's mouth. Teeth clattering, he trudged the bottom of the gulch, arms wrapped tight against his chest, avoiding the shadows, determined to reach the town of Deadwood and rob that bank, though he wanted to sit a spell. As inspiration for not doing so, he kept thinking Pa never raised no sissy. But Earl also thought that if he weren't no sissy, why did he notice those flowers along the stream?

Out of boredom or for whatever reason of impracticality, he mentioned the flowers to Claude, noting the white petals dangling over pine needles and aspen leaves green or brown, black and gold, a pleasing kaleidoscope.

Claude's reply consisted of disdain that made Earl shake his head at himself. Real men stocked interest in manlier things. They valued a half-side of pork-ribs or a wanton female, driving cattle. Or, and especially, crimson juice. A fella could get lost looking for too long at a congealing pool, how the pool turned into a purplish hue in twilight and shiny red in the afternoon. Always thick yet spreadable. Why, a couple drops smeared over a whole slice of toast. Slick, too. Earl rubbed the pad of his forefinger over that of his thumb then wiped his lips free of saliva and patted his gut while peering at the top of the gulch.

The sun had dipped below the treetops. Sheer mesmerizing it was, flaring yellow in the center, a white halo burn—

He lurched, having wandered into the stream, and staggered like a drunkard navigating stairs. Except instead of rickety wood creaking, water splashed and pebbles crunched. A mossy rock upended him. The fall cost him a bruised knee, scratched palms, and heated cheeks; his torso, arms, and knees wet. Earl got up, disgusted. Hell, he was no footman, a soldier able to do without a horse.

Could sure use that sit.

The charger, he recalled, had needed a break and, as a result, the steed laid dead. Wolves probably fed on its corpse, the lucky bastards. Another dunderheaded decision, his walking away from hoss-meat. Had he lingered, he could have sliced himself off a nice and juicy piece or three and cooked— Earl fingered his shirt pocket. Just as well he lit out after shooting the cursed beast seeing he had spent the last match starting the fire in the cabin.

"Idjut," jeered the specter Claude, "ya coulda ate the hoss raw."

Earl raised an eyebrow and scratched at the matted hairs along the nape of his neck.

Claude snorted. "Don't take on the look of a dumbstruck cow, feignin' ignorance over what I'm sayin'. Ya thought a somethin' eviler earlier." The specter's jeer turned into a knowing leer. "Din't ya?"

The lump in Earl's throat refused to be swallowed no matter how hard he gulped.

"Wade, that there clod in yer craw ain't 'cause o' thirst. Nor is the emptiness in yer gut due ta a thing 'cept hunger. Ya *need* ta *eat!* Can't be robbin' no blasted bank too weak fer aimin' yer guns." The specter threw up his hands. "Twice, boy, *twice* food was right there and both times ya up and run off. Why, Wade?"

Earl's toes had become numb. The stream was damming along the tip of his boot and seeping into a hole. He took a true accounting of himself for the first time in a month of Sundays. Filthy, tired to the bone, and penniless. A man could afford losing so much—

"'Fore he loses his self-worth, Wade. Isn't that what happened with her? Tryin' to live by the law. See the reward it got ya. 'Cause of—"

"Shad-up. Don't utter her name."

"Is yer dander up?" Claude snickered. "Thought she might erase the sins of yer father and heal yer soul. Called her Sweet Mary. Inn't that—?"

The sharp report of Earl's gun echoed throughout the gulch. The bullet going through Claude ricocheted off a boulder and sprayed rock-dust. A thin wisp of smoke trailed from the end of the Colt.

"Can't be shootin' me, Wade. I'm a whatchamacallit. Specter, 'member?"

Earl hung his head.

"Tell me o' Sweet Mary. Make me *feel* it."

Earl stowed his Colt. "I been courtin' Death ever since Sweet Mary's murder. She was the solitary person I ever gave a damn fer, my one bright spot. Leastways, black is how others see me. 'Earl C. Wade', they said and still say taday, 'ya ain't nothin' 'cept pitch-dark.' But somethin' in me changed when I fell in love. Me and her, we lived at the homestead with Ma and Pa.

"Plumb out the blue, Pa vanishes. Six months pass or however long 'fore he shows hisself again. Only person has an inkling of his bein' around is me. He's hidin', see. From what I don't know. Din't care." Earl paused and stroked his holster. He gazed ahead where the stream passed from sunlight and into shadow. "When I visited Pa in the cave he'd holed up in, he harped how his boy was outdoin' his accomplishments 'cause his boy's gotta job. Chump I was, paying no mind ta his anger.

"One particular evenin' I get home after laborin' at the sawmill. Homestead is quiet, so I holler names. Ain't nobody answerin' me and I creep through the house with the hairs on my arms standin' on end. Each room is empty, but the air, it's heavy, as if'n someone's died and Death ain't done lurkin'.

"I get ta the house's rear and slip inside mine and Mary's bedroom. Naked atop our bed Sweet Mary" —Earl gulped— "She...blood spilt out her puh—from twixt her legs, and Ma laid there on the floor, axe in her back, dress a torn-up mess. I guess Ma tried stoppin' Pa from humpin' my beloved and that angered 'im." Earl huffed. "What I do know is someone saw me and I lit out fast to save my neck. Always got the blame for stuff I never did. Been runnin' ever since." Breathing came difficult. Earl hit himself in the chest. "Ya hearin' me, Claude?"

"Yah, but I wonder. If'n ya been courtin' Death lo' these many months, why ain't ya settled in a cozy spot six feet unner?"

"Whenever the sumbitch knocks, I never invite it in. Guess I favor killin' too much."

"Ya sound better. Lighter afoot? More yerself?"

He nodded.

"Good. Now that yer melancholy is uprooted and ya stopped lookin' skyward fer the pearly gates, we oughta get goin' and find a spot to hole up. Kill and eat somethin'."

Again, Earl nodded, and ambled along the gulch as night conquered day. The gulch ended; the stream widened. Sticking by the gurgling water, he ducked beneath low-hanging branches and otherwise pushed his way, staying out of the woods where seeing came harder. He began to dry, but his shivers stayed. Not for the first time he rubbed his numb cheeks and glared at Claude.

The specter was as ever, gliding along, immune to temperatures or discomfort of rubbery legs and sore feet. On the few occasions Earl contemplated stopping for the night and building a shanty, Claude shot him a look.

"Not here. We gotsta find cover, somethin' fer ya craw."

Yessir, Earl knew how important food rated, that while settling in for the night tempted no less than one of them sireens, sleeping here meant waking cold. Frozen as the ice on the sides of the stream verging on being a river and leading across a plateau where cliffs forced Earl away from the rapids and into the woods. A bear's roar spawned greater shivers than did the frigid temperature. Earl freed his Colts, readying his trigger-fingers in case the bear spotted him and deemed him a tasty treat. Ole Claude, *he* had nary a concern over becoming a snack. Earl got an inkling death might be an improvement over being alive. Still, Claude missed earthly pleasures. A poor specter couldn't relish a baked pie, quaff a pint of beer, or have sour-mash set his gut aflame. Nope, on second thought—Earl tripped and toppled. His chin snapped shut when it hit the forest floor and sent starbursts through his head, the fall causing him to fire his Colts.

"Gawdammit," he moaned and spat. "Gawd...*damn*...*it!*"

"Wade," Claude hollered, "holster them guns 'fore ya shoot yer head clean off."

Earl struggled to one knee, gulping air. He holstered his pistols and went to stand. His knees popped. So did his back. After brushing off pine needles, he headed towards the river, whispering, "Tallyho"—a word he learned courtesy of a fancy-dressed Brit during a fox hunt. Claude and he weren't chasing a wily mutt, true enough, but Earl was hunting...*something* and wondered what. Riches and fame were well and fine, but flesh...For pleasure or feed? Those things and more.

The river ran off a precipice, the waterfall deafening. Across the ravine a shaft house catered to one side, its drainage pipe slanting into a gully; a nice spot for miner shacks since walls that tall blockaded winds. He sidestepped to manage the descent and strolled to a turn in the ravine.

Leaves and needles had piled inside a sluice that had not operated in months.

"Claude," he said, eyeing a moonlit partial roof, "ain't hide nor hair here."

A wolf howled gloomy and eerie, bowel-cramping. Earl re-drew his Colts. Where one wolf roamed, a pack followed. He crouched, straining to hear the snapping of twigs, and spotted nothing in his scouring of the ravine's ridges. The wolf's howl faded. Earl willed himself to go on.

Ahead were four cabins; three in ruins.

An age-weathered voice came through an open doorway. "If that wolf wanted ya, it'd done be too late. I oughta knows. Been huntin' Haska Wanagi goin' on years and seen him get more'n a few." A hand extended outward and waved inward. "Home ain't much, but yer welcome to hunker 'side my fire."

IV

HASKA WANAGI

Inside the shack Earl hunkered on an overturned bucket in front of a campfire, its smoke funneling to holes in the roof. Littered around him and his hospitable old host was hoary mining gear. Pickaxes, pans, hammers, several items too rusted or broken to recognize.

The old man squatted on the busted floor on the other side of the fire and sipped java from a dinted cup. He offered Earl the steaming coffee, but Earl declined, judging the contents too muddy.

"Have it yer way, mister, but why you decline is beyond me, temp bein' colder than a bared witch's wet cunt in Jan'ary." The old man poked a stirring stick into a pot of beans suspended by a tripod soot-encrusted at the top. Beans spilled over the rim and onto the embers.

Earl's stomach shriveled. "Wah, watch ya call the wolf?"

The old man regarded him through saggy eyelids, stroking his chest-length beard stained yellow at the ends. "Haska Wanagi. Lakota for white soul." He sniffled and rubbed the back of his hand under a bulbous nose. "That wolf be as pure-lookin' as the snow to come. Heaps. Count on it. Be droppin' through the holes." The old man exposed his neck peering up.

Chewy entered Earl's mind as he watched skin from the old man's jowls dangle. "Why do ya say heaps o' snow?"

"The air, she's damp, always a harbinger of snow. That and my rheumatism says Mother Nature is in an ornery mood." The old man looked to Earl. "Folks call me Mountain Bill, but I prefer William. Hah! Highfalutin."

"Sure-sure." Earl fisted and unfurled his hands several times, exercised life into them. "Yer mighty friendly. I wun't expected it."

The old goat moved slow, picking up a rusted spoon and dipping into the beans. He blew on the spoonful and shoved it in his mouth. Munched and talked at the same time. "I sees no point in mistrustin' a man straight away." He gulped and wiped his lips. "Had ya gone on out the gulch, ya'd found suspicion by runnin' inta Statler and the others. Small town up ahead. Not even that to be honest."

Earl inspected the cabin for signs of another occupant. A single bedroll was at the wall sporting the smallest spaces between the boards. Claude hovered there; his arms crossed, fingers drumming. "Any ever visit ya?"

"Nah. Me and Statler, we don't get along. Hell-on-wheels him. Unofficial leader for the thirteen of us hangin' onto these Hills after our mine went belly-up. Ain't much, Deadwood Gulch; fewer alive every year there, but those still kickin' are stubborn and dyin' to hit pay-dirt. Most what they pan is flakes out the streams. Bare enough to keep themselves in clothin's. Oh, they dig for veins, but ain't no mother-lode these days. She died out. Gone in way lotsa things vanish. I had thoughts of doin' that but got no family or nothin'. So I scout Haska Wanagi and hunt other critters." The old man gestured over his shoulder to a long-barreled firearm leaning next to a tarp-covered window.

Earl draped a forearm across his thighs. His other hand he hung a thumb's breadth from the Colt. "Purty stock on that Sharps. Ya buff her?"

"Oh yah. Not much to do. Others residin' in Deadwood Gulch, they're younger. Don't cater much to playin' cards except Poker and use matchsticks in place of money. What's the point?"

"None, I reckon. Deadwood Gulch far off?"

Mountain Bill bent forward, his buckskin coat shifting and revealing a bone-handled knife sheathed at his hip. "Keep on the direction ya were goin'. Ravine lets out within eye-shot of the Gulch. Sure ya want no beans?"

Earl's top lip curled.

"What'd ya say yer name was?"

"Wade." He watched Claude drag an extended thumb across his throat.

Bill spooned another bite. "Can't say as I know the name. Where ya from?"

"Arizona territory," he lied.

"What ya doin' here so far north in the Dakotas?"

Earl opened his mouth, closed it; demanded his ground-to-a-halt mind concoct an explanation. The claim of being a prospector was ludicrous. Too, he could be considered neither a rancher nor farmhand. A gambler out on his luck whose hoss died on him? He twisted to the doorway, as if in seeing outside he would sight an answer. A shadow blackened a thin layer of snow. The shadow disappeared upon the wind gusting. Treetop, Earl guessed, and turned his attention back to the old man. He drew a Colt. Spent every ounce of self-control to deny his urge to squeeze the trigger. "Don't go for that bone-handled skinner attached to yer hip."

Mountain Bill gulped, spoon slipping from his grasp. The hand that held his silverware remained aloft and trembled. "What's the meanin' of this?"

Earl rose and kept his gun trained on Bill. After going around to stand behind the old man, he put the barrel to the back of the old man's head. "Claude?"

"Who's"—Bill gasped—"that?"

"Wade," the specter said, "ain't I been tellin' ya what needs done?"

"Uh-huh. I need ta eat."

"Then eat," gushed the old man. "Granted, I got just the beans, but have them. Every last one! Help yerself. Ain't got much, true enough, but take it! Whatever ya want."

Flesh...

Earl bent at the waist and wrapped an arm around Bill's throat. He squeezed, trying to crush the windpipe of the old man pitching a fit. Beans hit Earl in the face when Bill's desperate kicks for life knocked over the tripod and sent the cooking pot flying. Embers from the fire sparked and rose; rapidly at first, then slowing, mirroring Bill's struggle to breathe, his franticness eventually stopping. Earl let the old man slip from his grasp. Quick rooting got him the old man's knife. Its marred blade was four or five inches in length and back-curved, wide at the hilt. A blade designed for skinning.

"Get on 'im," Claude urged.

He sat on the old man's torso, straddling his ribs and shaking while holstering the Colt. For the zeal killing had wrought, he was weaker than a new-born kitten. The middle of his chest flared in pain. Why he didn't know. His breathing was normal.

A lot better than Mountain Bill's.

Earl chuckled and parted the old man's coat. He scooted back, enjoying the stiffening rod in his own britches, and ripped open Bill's shirt. Used the knife to flick a hairy, saggy tit. Earl's dick twitched, stomach rumbled.

Claude glided in front of the window beside the Sharps. His voice was husky, smooth. "Like yer first time fuckin', inn't it? Waitin' so long, wonderin' if'n ya oughta, thinkin' it's wrong yet knowin' watch ya want is right. Ain't nothin' better than rammin' a glistenin' pussy or eatin' a man. These desires, they yer instincts. Ya has no choice satisfyin' 'em."

"Nope," Earl panted. "I ain't."

"Jam the steel right in there. C'mon. Yer already bound for Hell. Sooner or later, them hounds will catch up and take yer soul to the burnin' pits. Might as well make yer remainin' days count, yessir! Go on now. Eat yer fill. Ya deserve it. Starvin', hunted. Heartache 'n losses. Sweet Mary. Time ya got yers. Inn't it?"

"Uh-huh."

"Then reap the flesh, Wade!"

The dull blade and Earl's weakness made cutting the tit difficult. Between sallow edges of skin lay a mixture of pink, red, and yellow. Earl raised the cut-off piece of meat to his nose and sniffed, extended his tongue to lick. He shuddered.

And chomped.

Scratching noises sounded behind him. He turned slow, ginger, Bill's flesh draping his chin. His eyes locked onto the wolf's the moment Haska Wanagi leapt. Earl went for his holstered Colt too late for shooting the wolf. Its heavy body airborne knocked him over. No chance to do anything but grapple fur to keep those giant teeth from ripping his gullet.

God Almighty, why did he put away his gun? Claude, telling him to eat, to cut...

He jammed the old man's knife in the wolf's neck. Haska Wanagi yelped; so did he.

Nips took pieces of Earl's neck and face. Paws dug at his legs and gut. In an act of desperation, Earl released the knife and the wolf. He forced his forearm under the wolf's throat and pushed up, fumbling for his pistol with his neck rent and cheek flat against the floor. His hand gripped the Colt. He aimed the barrel upward, pulled the trigger.

The wolf howled and slumped off.

He scrambled up, swiping at his face, screaming, "Claude, Claude!" and wondering whether the wolf was dead.

A low and guttural growl filled the cabin. He whimpered, backing towards the wall where the Sharps rifle leaned, where Claude had been floating but wasn't anymore. Earl rubbed at his eyes. Through a splitting film of red gleamed something white.

The whiteness blurred.

Comin' fer me, he shouted in silence.

With both guns raised, he fired. The wolf's howls joined the barking of his revolvers. Bullets hit the beast — they had to; from that distance he couldn't miss — but it again launched at him, crashing into and hurtling Earl. He burst through the wall and glimpsed treetops, chunks of board.

Light burst inside his head when it slammed against the ground. Haska Wanagi landed atop him, unmoving. Earl tried to lift the animal. No use. He wasn't going anywhere soon. Tired to the bone.

Hell with it.

He shut his eyes on the cascading snowflakes and passed out.

KIMIMELA

Earl came-to a fraction at a time, memory-dreams flashing through his mind's eye. He saw himself as a boy fleeing from Pa, scampering to avoid a whiplashing for setting flame to a neighbor's home. There he was as a teen dipping his tally-whacker into an overweight and lonesome woman, the apish wife of that same neighbor. Then came Sweet Mary smiling at him. He had just asked her to marry him. Beauty begot ugliness. She faded away and an image of Pa replaced her. He and Earl were in the kitchen, Pa looking out the window and grousing on his son's latest screw-up while Earl aimed his gun.

Other memories came and went, but that particular one he wanted to wring for every detail because he hadn't before recalled shooting Pa. The more he grabbed onto the wisp, the faster it slipped away, getting chased off for good by something soft brushing over creaky floorboards. The whisking stopped. Then came liquid pouring into porcelain. Dishes clinked. Earl sniffed.

Horseradish.

And dust that tickled his nose.

Bad prospect, sneezing and racking his ribs that were sore enough, he wondered whether a wagon had run over him. An ugly sight to behold if so. He thought to check, but the effort of peeking was too much, the temptation to go back asleep undeniable.

Not until wet cloth dampened his forehead did he open his eyes to lock gazes with a Lakota, her irises tawny pools.

"C'mon, Earl," they glinted. "Swim in us."

He would have if not for the rest of her. Chocolate-colored hair draped her wide, copper face. He liked the softness of her chin, the suppleness of her neck. To see more, he pressed his head against the pillow. That hurt, but was worth the pain. She had to bend farther to dab his forehead, which caused the beige dress to droop at the bustline and reveal her modest cleavage. Small breasts rated fine to him if round and pert, and hers were.

Now those apples he could munch.

Easy to cut, he bet, and imagined how juicier her tit was compared to the old man's. Saltier and fattier. He rent his gaze up, returning to the woman's eyes to go swimming anew in those tawny pools.

Her jaw dropped. Almond-shaped eyelids spread apart. The metal tray she carried clanged on the floor. She held palms a pinkish shade out in front of her. Tiny steps whisked the woman to the room's door hanging by a single hinge.

"Wasin-ee-coo," she gasped, then again whispered that funny word.

Earl's "Hey" to keep her from going died as he rose on his elbows.

Unwise, moving. Walls closed in on him. He swallowed, tried to ignore his gut churning by focusing on the silver tray the Lakota had dropped, a tin pitcher and muddy paste in a clay jar on its side while the room spun. He begged it not to pick up speed, but the room spurned him and went into fast loop-dee-doo's. His arms slipped from under him and his head hit the feathery pillow.

Pain fired in his temples.

Darkness came.

He later awakened to constant tapping and blinked at the tattered ceiling until it came into focus. Only then did he venture locating the source of that incessant noise-making.

Across the room a bear leaned against furniture. Dresser? Hard to say with his vision blurred other than in the middle. Wait. A bear? Earl looked again and realized the glob of fur was a mountain-man wearing a hide. Impossible to tell where that pelt stopped and the man's beard started. Too similar in color.

The mountain-man pointed at Earl. "Yer'er num'er bur'er, were'er?"

What? Earl shook his head. Another mistake. Unconsciousness revisited him.

Confusion over his whereabouts clouded Earl's thinking upon reawakening, unable to recollect how he had gotten here inside this shabby room and on this saggy bed resting on his side instead of his back—a sleeping-position he hadn't taken since harming that shoulder after the branch he hung from broke.

The pillow tugged at his face when he rolled. He touched his cheek. Found something hard and crusty. Blood? Soft cloth above that. A bandage, he reckoned, and licked his chapped lips with a sandy tongue, stared unthinking. After a spell, he got his elbows beneath him and studied faded yellow wallcovering. Cobwebs strung in the room's corner. A busted drawer lay in front of a pair of deerskin boots that led to furry britches and a shirt, coat.

"Statler." The mountain-man jabbed a thumb at his own beefy chest before pointing it at Earl. "Your name?"

"Wade."

Statler walked to the bed, his heavy footsteps making Earl grimace. Steeliness braced the man's blue eyes set in an angular face, nose mushed. If Statler's mien ever showed kindness, his smirk buried it. The way he glowered...

Earl dropped his gaze and spotted ivory pistol handles. "Ya from the Cavalry?"

"Why you asking?"

"Yer gun-butts are out. Only folk I know draw crossways serve in the military."

"That's uh, a helluva thing to note after wakening, especially for someone with a banged-up head who's been in-and-out a couple days." Statler took a step back. "Been debate betwixt us here in the Gulch whether you're a man off on luck or the monster Kimimela says."

"Who?"

"Kimimela. The woman dressed your head and tried to doctor you 'til she got spooked."

"The Injun?"

"I dislike that word. You much as whisper red nigger, I'll kill you."

"Fair enough. Why she call me a monster? I ain't done nothin'."

"We'll see. Suppose you were just walking through these rough mountains for no good reason and happened to stumble onto ole Bill. Sat with him to eat beans, which is what you were doing when a tribe attacked."

"Where'd ya get that notion? Weren't no tribe but a wolf. Them who rescued me had ta see it. Landed on top o' me. Couldn't move it."

"Mister, I was among those who saved you. Only things of note we found were you unconscious, your mouth smeared in blood and guns scattered, moccasin tracks, a wall busted through, and Bill with his shirt torn open. You know anything regarding his missing tit?"

Moccasin tracks? No wolf carcass? Earl gulped. "I'm tellin' ya, we got 'tacked. Wuh, William called the beast Ha, Haska Wanagi."

Statler harrumphed. "Perchance Kimimela was right, you being a wasi'cu."

"Wassee-huh?"

"Lakota name for a beast-spirit that takes over a person so mad with greed, they hunger for flesh." Statler tapped his forefinger on a pistol's butt. "Kimimela says you had the same look in your eyne her chief did after he went lust-crazy for blood and members of her clan began vanishing. Few remained when they figured out who was behind the slaughters."

"They kill the chief?"

"Nope. Haska Wanagi disappeared before they could put an arrow through his heart. Searched for months. Legend has it a wasi'cu can change into a wolf. Bill believed it lock, stock, and barrel. That's why he was out there, to stop Wanagi from killing again. Me and Bill, we argued hard over that foolishness. Now I think myself the dupe."

"Watch ya mean?"

"We'll see. First tell me why you were filthy head-to-foot but your guns were sparkling clean. You took care of them. Too good."

"Sayin' I'm a gunslinger?"

"I'm not saying what you are because I don't know. Yet. Aim to find out, though. Kimimela sees a beast inside you, but me, what I notice is blackness. A sky of it."

Earl nodded. "Since you'uns don't approve o' me, how 'bout I get on outa here?"

"Ain't that simple. You're too weak. That and Mother Nature opened her ass and shat white on us. Has us snowed-in for weeks 'lessin we snowshoe to Deadwood, and ain't no one getting that far in this weather. Even were it summer, I wouldn't let you. Not until I learn a few things."

"Such as?"

Statler tromped to the door. "Several days from now I'll return. In the meantime, once the snow stops, I'm going to investigate Bill's cabin. Pray what I find inside it—wolf hair, paw prints, scratch marks, whatever else—goes in your favor. If not, I'm bringing an axe-handle. You getting hit a few times, me breaking your bones, will ensure your honesty." He pointed at a row of three windows on Earl's left. "You're on the second floor of an old saloon, closed since the mine went belly-up. Attempt to leave and you'll run into men downstairs armed and ready to shoot."

"Sumbitch, can't keep me prisoner. Hear me?!" He bit his lips to keep from bellowing, "I'll put a slug in every one o' ya!"

VI

CLAUDE-PA

Snowed the next day. And the one after that. The following. For five running, the sky sprinkled. Earl spent the first pacing his room, working on inventing a way to get free of his prison. Once he snuck to check on the watchers below. Boards creaking announced each feather-step he took to the bannister. Two men glared up and waved the ends of their double-barrel shotguns. If he attempted an escape, the guards would pepper the walls with his blood. Earl moseyed back to the bed, rubbing his forearms, and cloaked himself with the tattered blanket.

On the second day his stomach developed a knot. A nuisance in the beginning, the hole in his gut became a pit he tried filling with saliva. The spit failed to lessen his ready-to-get-sick feeling and the cavern expanded to the size of a blown-out volcano. He knew of those craters because he'd studied one in a big-city newspaper. The article, best he gathered, described an eruption far south of the States.

Mexico or Barkill.

Nah, that wasn't right. Hard to think with his stomach feeding on itself. Was the name Barful? Barzul? Brazil! He had heard tell cannibals ate sacrificed folk.

Lucky sumbitches.

To keep his mind from conjuring images of dead virgins ripe for tasting, he stood at the window and gaped. Not that outside offered much distraction. Mother Nature's defecation hid everything except pines, aspens, and buildings. Even those dumped intermittent fluffs of powder when the wind blew strong.

Too long staring at that scenery and Earl understood what snow-blind meant.

The second night ranked worse than the first. In the dark it was unavoidable contemplating Statler's making good on his threat of torture. The leader of Deadwood Gulch loomed big as a giant in Earl's imagination and he shivered picturing the mountain-man's shadow falling on him.

Branches snapping due to an overload of snow set his nerves further on edge, were reminiscent of bones breaking.

Daybreak again, the blizzard kept on. Exhaustion teamed with starvation and thirst to create hallucinations. He saw Sweet Mary, Ma, various people he'd killed. Last came Mountain Bill. Pa, blessed be the maker, went unrepresented. Neither did Claude appear, whose absence weighed on Earl. The specter had a talent for words and bringing smiles, though grinning would hurt with his lips fissured dunes.

He traipsed to the banister and croak-begged the guards for water. Their laughing gave him little choice except go to a window and tug. The frame slid, its wood grinding dirt. He scooped handfuls of snow into his mouth. After kind of sating his thirst, he pushed on the window's bottom sill. The window shut until an inch of space remained. There it halted. He yanked on the top to no avail.

The room's frigid temperature plummeted.

Third night melded into the fourth day. That eve Earl awoke with a start. Glasses tinkling and rowdy laughter filled his ears. The room fresher yet sweltering reeked of sweat and booze. Across it a naked whore brushed her golden hair in front of a new dresser backed by a spotless mirror. In shifting her hips, one cheek of her ass flattened while the other rounded. He traced her curves, admired the slope of her shoulders. Via the reflection she gave him a sexy half-grin.

He rubbed his eyes.

The woman was no more and the saloon returned to a decrepit state. If Earl's mouth had been dry before, it was now desert and no amount of sucking in air filled his chest.

A nightmare, he thought, and waited for sleep.

Still, bottles clinked against glasses and drunken men bellowed loud enough to be inaudible. Hours passed and those sounds remained, just beyond hearing, a continual buzz that could drive a fella mad. Later he plastered his palms against the sides of his head and searched for something thin and sharp to pop his eardrums.

There was nothing to use.

Day five delivered parted clouds. Sunlight flared between white fluffs to paint the horizon yellow. Snow-crystals sparkled in that light and it seemed to Earl the world was rebirthing, its sins erased. While he looked, his shivers intensified. From a raging fever. The volcano in his gut erupted and his ass leaked noxious gas. He wrapped his arms around himself, rocked. Did his eyes water? He wondered at that, how it could be after he had drank so little for so long.

"Claude," he said, his teeth clacking, "where the hell are ya?"

"Here," the specter replied, bare-visible in the far corner. "Nearin' the end, Wade. Might wanna spill the truth 'fore it's too late."

"Watch ya mean?"

"Fibbed ta me. Yer Pa was a couple years dead and buried when Sweet Mary met her fate." The specter glided from the shadows. "C'mon now. Can't bullshit me. I was there watchin'. Best come clean on the rest."

"Why—?" Whatever Earl meant to say he forgot. Cramps infested his gut, as if someone had latched onto his innards and twisted.

Claude sighed and shook his head. "That day ya came home from the sawmill pissed off. Foreman busted yer chops. Mary by then weren't sweet, was she? Nah. Grew tired of yer bullshit, the lyin' over the whore ya fucked on the side."

"Shad-up."

"No bitch has a right slappin' a man, huh? Ya dragged her to the bed and raped her, din't ya, ta teach the cunt a lesson."

"Lies," Earl shouted. "Damned and dirty falsehoods." He closed his eyes and groaned, fearing whatever his innards had gotten to percolate.

"Think on it. Mary's pussy dry and bleedin' after ya spurt yer wad. Weepin' she was. Ah, Wade, ya hated that." Claude's voice changed from nasal-sounding to guttural. "Was a weakness, *boy*, I lashed out o' ya."

A stream of foul, brown liquid exploded up from Earl's belly and out his mouth. When he finished upheaving off the bed's side, he confirmed his worst nightmare had taken Claude's place. Pa taller and broader built, roundish nose, dimpled chin. A scar traveled from his forehead to his forever-arcing upper lip.

"Ya shot Sweet Mary," Pa carried on. "Bam! Right betwixt her tits. Recollect that, boy? How Ma came runnin' and when she saw what ya did, she came back with a woodchopper. Ya put a fist to Ma's jaw. Put that bible-thumping bitch on her ass quick. She dropped the axe 'n ya snatched it up. Kicked her 'til she flopped. Fish on a bank. That's what you thought. Then ya buried that axe in her back. Told Claude ya ran on account of bein' innocent. That, boy, is somethin' ya never been or will be. A coward, though. Shot yer pappy while he was lookin' out the winduh. Get ready for payback."

Earl curled up next to the headboard. He wanted to cover his eyes, his ears. Couldn't bring himself to move. Frightened to the bone.

But staying still was okay.

Pa began to fade.

Except...

Through Pa's disappearing Earl saw something...

Large. Furry. Running.

Statler.

Who used his right hand to smack an axe handle in the opposite palm.

"Let's hear it, what happened to Mountain Bill."

"Beans," Earl blubbered. "Eatin' beans when Haska Wanagi got after us."

"You're lying." Statler reached inside his coat and threw a piece of skin onto the bed. "Bill's tit got cut off, not bitten, and those markings aren't from a wolf."

"No idea watch—"

Statler swung. The axe handle hissed on its way to hitting Earl's thigh. Either the weapon or Earl's bone cracked. He screamed and almost dodged the next swing that crashed into his hip. Another belted the small of his spine.

"Beans," he shrieked. "Eatin' 'em! Hasa—" He scampered across the mattress, stood.

And got struck in the gut.

A pinch in his chest. Bile in his gullet. He dropped to his hands and knees, sobbing, and crawled for the doorway. Those guards didn't matter anymore. Time to worry over them was when they aimed their shotguns at him. If he could just—

Statler clubbed the middle of his back. The scream that tore at Earl's throat could have been a woman's until it was silenced by more punishment, beating, bashing. His limbs gave out. He lay with his face to the floor, coughing blood and staring at the banister, mesmerized because it changed, darkened, slithered. Lacquered wood sprouted bark. Between the pegs, he saw walls flicker.

Just as Pa vanished, so did the saloon.

Blue sky peeked through the forest ceiling. Mist and fog swirled over the ground. Not far off beat many drums and over that drumming, a chant.

"Hey-ya. Hey-ya."

Earl scrambled to his feet, baffled, went to draw a Colt. His holster wasn't there.

"Bust a move." Pa's voice sounded from nowhere and everywhere. "Comeuppance."

He whirled upon heel.

"Now, boy, ain't like when you killed that posse. Can't harm what's comin'."

A howl equal parts wolf, bear, and puma sent Earl scuttling.

VII

WASI'CU

Indian-drumming boomed throughout the forest, but that wasn't the only sound terrifying Earl. Twigs snapped and fallen branches crunched soon after his passing. If he closed his mouth, he still heard panting, the sort a beast made. This while paws stomped the ground.

Faster, he urged himself.

More drumming; the Lakota, his feet, those of the beast. He hurdled and burst through shrubbery, jumped streams and swam across rivers. Sometimes war-painted faces poked from the bushes lining banks. He did not understand the gibberish those Lakota spoke, but got the distinct impression they chided and ridiculed, accused him of being a flesh-eater. That was true—no denying it after the crimes committed—and he felt awash in shame, sobbing and begging the divine for clemency.

Other times, when he turned sharp or dared to glance over his shoulder, he spotted the wasi'cu. Taller than any grizzly, the fur of its man-shaped body colored ash. Ram-horns rose from its wolf-shaped and skinless head. Human bones tied together for makeshift torso-armor rattled. A skull draping its groin bobbed.

His ability to note such detail meant the wasi'cu had gotten too close.

Earl sped up, unknowing from where he gained that extra oomph which blurred the foliage. Whatever reason or source, he was grateful for it. The noise of the wasi'cu quieted, but never silenced. The beast kept chasing then, as he scampered around trees and jumped over boulders, stumbled here and there, skirted the occasional cave that seemed a good hiding place if not for being a death-trap. Pa said there was no harming the animal. Couldn't hide from it either. His journeying from the netherworld showed Earl spirit-beings witnessed all.

So he had no choice, had to run and keep running, but damn, fleeing came hard after a man's legs numbed and a hellish fire scorched his lungs and that cramp atop his ribs demanded a respite, whispering insistent it was okay for him to stop here in this clearing where he had plenty of warning to take off again should the wasi'cu near.

Lies.

Damned and dirty falsehoods.

He knew that.

And halted regardless.

Put both palms on his knees. Spit drained from his mouth. Belly heaved. It was only after throwing up Earl realized the drumming quit, that the wind tickling the nape of his neck was a breath, and the child whimpering weren't a kid but him.

"Please," he croaked. "*Purty* please."

A whip cracked before whizzing and cutting his back. Amid screaming, he dropped to bended knees.

Footfalls.

Scuffed boots flattened yellowish brown grass.

"Ya ain't crazy, boy. This here's the netherworld that keeps enterin' yer mind. Anythin' is possible. Figure out how ya got here? Little by little, boy, greed consumed ya. Pussy, money, killin'. Fine in the beginnin' but after so long, just flesh can quench the thirst. That monster chasin' ya is part o' ya. Even afore Haska Wanagi attacked. Realize what I'm sayin' means?"

The bullwhip's feathered popper drew lazy circles on the ground, causing the dead blades to break or bend and Earl to pout.

"Cry-baby. Everythin' is a matter a mind, includin' what limits ya. Wasn't luck saved ya from hangin'. Remember it, boy. *Picture* dangling, life leavin'. Ya crossed ta the other side. Leastways long enough ta become more than afore. Came back ta the real world and grabbed that rope, hauled yerself up 'nough ta loosen the noose and fall. Branch never broke. Ain't no rascal ever drew walked so fortunate as ta have that happen.

"Now here ya are again with us spirits, this time while Statler abuses yer body. Ain't ya tired of gettin' whipped?"

Sick of it to his marrow. For as long as he could recall, folk had been kicking his ass.

"Hightail to the livin', boy. Set to killin' and eatin'. What ya were meant to do."

He peeked to find Pa gone. The wasi'cu stared back. Its canine snout opened and blocked out its irises of blue. Slobber and hot breath stinking of rotten meat hit Earl in the face. He closed his eyes and waited.

Moments passed.

The bite didn't happen.

When he relooked, the bannister interrupted his view of the saloon wall beyond. The axe handle swooshed. Earl spat a mouthful of blood and rolled over in time to grab Statler's weapon. He stood, snickering at the mountain-man's jaw hanging, his gawping.

"Yer supposed ta be dying," claimed that expression.

But he wasn't.

No, Earl C. Wade was alive and dandy.

"I'm gonna kill ya, Statler. After that, devour ya." He tipped his head towards the lobby where the guards scrambled for the stairs. "Them as well. Save your Injun bitch whore for last. Uh-huh. I spy everythin'. You weak and frail, hopin' she'd say yes to yer proposing. Know I'll shove my cock deep in Kimimela and choke the shit out o' her while I shoot my wad. Then eat her, too. 'Cept she'll be alive 'til the bitter end."

Prospects which got him right hard.

JOIN MY STREET TEAM

What's a street team? A group of fans that support an author by getting the word out about the author's publications. This is done via social media platforms. Word-of-mouth (or media-of-mouth) is any author's greatest tool, especially in today's publishing world. Given the market is inundated with books on a daily basis, it's harder than ever for an author to get noticed. Without media/word-of-mouth, well, said author is about as dead in the water as a floating, bloated fish.

You're probably wondering what's in it for you. As a street team member you are first in line for advance reader copies and get sneak-peaks at upcoming publications. But that's not all. Members are eligible to win prizes from the promotions they join. Some of these prizes are amazing. How amazing? How about a First Edition Lord of the Rings trilogy? Others include free, signed Calasade paperbacks and gift cards from the store of their choice. Additional boons include participating in conversations with other fans, awarded swag (bookmarks, signed art, etc.), and personal interaction with Mark Stone. As if all the aforementioned isn't enough, members will receive exclusive autographed publications such as Calasade: Gilinard and Istel when the novella is complete. Shipped free of charge.

Register at authormarkstone.com.

SUBSCRIBER ADVANTAGES

Building a relationship with my readers is one of the most rewarding things about writing. Me, I'm a reader, too, so we share a love of books. On occasion I send recommendations of the best books I've read along with special offers to those who opt to get updates on my publications. On occasion I give out free books to them, too.

Register at authormarkstone.com.

FOR THE READER

LEAVE A REVIEW

MAKE A DIFFERENCE

Reviews are the single most important component for an author's success, so please leave a review on Amazon if you've liked what you read. Heck, even if you didn't. I strive to be the best writer I can. Any and all feedback will assist me in that.

To do this, go to my Amazon page:

amazon.com/author/calasade

And click on the book you've just read, then write a quick review of what you thought.

Thank you ever so much.

ABOUT MARK STONE

Mark Stone splits his time between the United States and Spain with his greatest inspiration, his wife. Having written award-winning Flash Fiction, he is now a novelist writing tales mostly of Ancient Roman Fantasy. He will venture into other genres, such as Weird Western and Historical Fiction.

Where to find him online:

twitter.com/calasade | facebook.com/Calasade

wordsbycalasade.com | authormarkstone.com

ALSO BY MARK STONE

NEVER STILL

Mark is always writing. Keep up to date with his publications by visiting authormarkstone.com.

COPYRIGHT